a song
in the
MIST

OXFORD
UNIVERSITY PRESS

Great Clarendon Street, Oxford OX2 6DP

Oxford University Press is a department of the University of Oxford.
It furthers the University's objective of excellence in research, scholarship,
and education by publishing worldwide. Oxford is a registered trade mark of
Oxford University Press in the UK and in certain other countries

First published 2021

British Library Cataloguing in Publication Data available

ISBN: 978-0-19-277207-7 (hardback)

1 3 5 7 9 10 8 6 4 2

Printed in China

Paper used in the production of this book is a natural, recyclable product made
from wood grown in sustainable forests. The manufacturing process conforms
to the environmental regulations of the country of origin

For Oswin.
With thanks to Helen,
for harmonizing on this 'song'
— C.A.

For Diana, a panda fan
— F.W.

'Where words fail, music speaks'
Hans Christian Andersen

A Song in the MIST

Corrinne Averiss   Fiona Woodcock

OXFORD
UNIVERSITY PRESS

Chi is hiding.
If you're quiet, if you're quick,
you might just see her.

Between conifer trees and bamboo leaves.
A shy panda bear.

Chi loves to listen.
Being silent brings sounds to her ears.

The swish of bamboo.
The chitter of tiny birds.

But today, something new.

Gentle, sweet, the air made musical.

It floats on the breeze, curls around trees,

makes a bridge over the water . . .

. . . and brings Chi to a little house.

Carefully she creeps,
as near as she dare,
closer to the sound.

Until she finds it.

A boy
who blows breath
through a piece of bamboo.

He stops.
He has seen her.

Chi runs . . .
as fast as her paws will scurry.

Into the cover of the forest.

Back to the safety of her tree.

And all is stillness, until . . .

Leaves crunch.
A twig snaps!

'Hello!'

'Where are you?'

Chi's heart beats fast.
Her paws grip the bark.

She follows quietly
from tree to tree.

But as the sun sets,
the air cools,

and mist begins
to fill the forest.

The boy stumbles, and his flute tumbles,
onto the forest floor . . .

Chi climbs down to look.
And as she looks, she hears a cry,

'Grandpa, help! I'm lost!'

If only she had the courage . . .

Just enough courage . . .

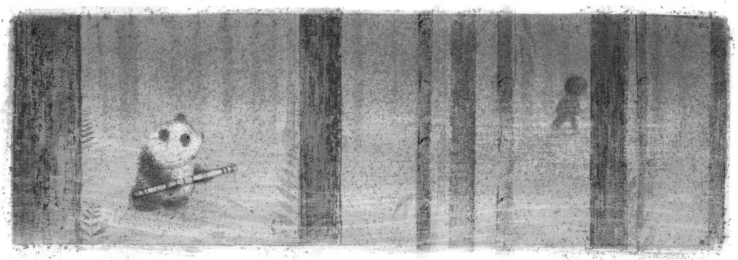

If only Chi could find the courage to . . .

The boy stops.
He follows the sound . . .

Chi beckons
him to climb . . .

To follow her, out of the
mist and ferns . . .

Up to where the moon shines bright
and the lights of Grandpa's house
twinkle in the distance.

Chi returns the boy's flute.
The boy understands.

And with breath and bamboo,
he sends a song into the mist.

It curls around trees, makes a bridge over the water . . .

. . . and tells Grandpa that help is needed.

Grandpa follows the song . . .

. . . all the way to their tree.

The boy smiles a *thank you* for Chi.
He holds out his flute.

Chi finds the courage to take it.
It must be time to say goodbye.

Chi watches the boy and Grandpa return home.
The forest feels alive with their invisible friendship.
Stars shine brighter. Fireflies glow warmer.

Branches seem to connect them,
as Chi holds tight to her precious bamboo gift.

At sunrise, a familiar song
wakes Chi from her sleep.

And this time, Chi bravely
sounds a note right back.

A friendship, suspended in the air,
between a panda and a boy.

Made only of breath and bamboo.